You Choose Stories: Wonder Woman
is published by Stone Arch Books,
A Capstone Imprint
1710 Roe Crest Drive
North Mankato, Minnesota 56003
www.capstonepub.com

STAR41678

Library of Congress Cataloging-in-Publication Data is
available on the Library of Congress website.
ISBN: 978-1-4965-8349-9 (library binding)
ISBN: 978-1-4965-8439-7 (paperback)
ISBN: 978-1-4965-8354-3 (eBook PDF)

Summary: The monsters of myth are about to take a
bite out of the Big Apple! Ares has unleashed the
Minotaur, and a host of other creatures, on New York City.
Now you must help Wonder Woman defend the city against
the God of War's *Myth Monster Mayhem!*

Editor: Christopher Harbo

Designer: Hilary Wacholz

Printed in the United States of America.
PA70

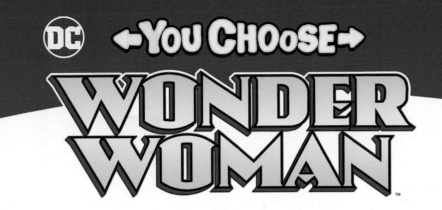

DC ←YOU CHOOSE→

WONDER WOMAN™

MYTH MONSTER MAYHEM

written by
Steve Korté

illustrated by
Omar Lozano

Wonder Woman created by
William Moulton Marston

STONE ARCH BOOKS
a capstone imprint

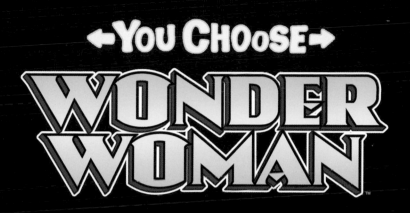

The monsters of myth are about to take a
bite out of the Big Apple! Ares has unleashed
the Minotaur, and a host of other creatures,
on New York City. Now you must help Wonder
Woman defend the city against the God of
War's *Myth Monster Mayhem!*

Follow the directions at the bottom of
each page. The choices YOU make will change
the outcome of the story. After you finish one
path, go back and read the others for more
Wonder Woman adventures!

CLANG!

The sound of crashing swords fills the air. As the sun shines in a cloudless sky, more than a dozen women battle each other on a grassy field near the ocean shore. All of the women are strong and athletic. They wear shining suits of metal armor. As each woman swings her sword, another quickly blocks it with her own weapon.

The women, known as Amazons, are training to improve their fighting skills. These mighty warriors, created centuries ago by the Greek gods, live together on a secret island. The island's name is Themyscira, and its beauty has earned it the nickname Paradise Island.

Although the Amazons have built a peaceful society on their island, one god is not happy that they were created. He is Ares, the God of War. He has battled the Amazons many times and vows that someday he will destroy them.

Turn the page.

So every day, the Amazons train to become stronger warriors. They need to be ready for the day when Ares attacks. And today, one Amazon practices her swordplay harder than the rest.

That Amazon is Princess Diana, the daughter of Queen Hippolyta. Diana is tall and strong. As she swings her sword, blocking every blow, she knows that she is not like the other Amazons.

Years ago, when a nuclear war threatened to destroy the world, the Amazons chose Princess Diana to be their champion. She traveled far from Themyscira and saved the world. In the process, she became the beloved hero known as Wonder Woman.

"Princess Diana!" a voice suddenly calls out.

The battle training comes to a stop. Diana removes her helmet, and her long black hair flows in the wind.

A troop of Amazon warriors marches across the sandy dunes and stops before Diana. She recognizes the Amazons as guards from the royal palace.

"Your Highness," says one of the guards.
"Your mother has requested your presence in
the palace. She says it's an emergency."

Diana quickly sheaths her sword and starts
running. Seconds later, she speeds through the
streets of Themyscira. She runs so fast that she
is practically a blur. No other Amazon can run
as fast as Diana.

The gleaming, white marble towers atop
Themyscira's palace come into view. Diana races
into the building and enters the main hall.

Her mother sits on the throne, surrounded by
other Amazons.

"Diana, I have very bad news," says Queen
Hippolyta. "The Minotaur has escaped from
Doom's Doorway."

Diana gasps. Doom's Doorway is a sealed door
on Themyscira. Behind that door lies a tunnel
that leads to some of the world's most dangerous
monsters. These creatures are chained to rocks
far below the island.

Turn the page.

The Minotaur is a giant creature with the head of a bull and the body of a man. It has razor-sharp teeth and a monstrous appetite. Many brave warriors have battled the Minotaur, only to be gobbled down by the hungry creature.

"Where is the Minotaur now?" asks Diana.

"It's been seen in New York City," says Queen Hippolyta.

The queen pauses and then starts to ask, "Diana, will you—"

"Of course, Mother," Diana replies before the queen can finish her sentence. "I will travel to New York to capture the Minotaur."

Diana races to the edge of Themyscira, where her personal aircraft stands ready for takeoff. Diana has many superpowers, including the ability to fly. But today she chooses to leave Themyscira in her incredibly fast Invisible Jet.

Diana reaches into a storage area beneath the jet and removes her star-spangled Wonder Woman uniform. In seconds, she dons her outfit.

Wonder Woman climbs into the jet's cockpit and immediately becomes invisible herself. Now she can fly quickly and quietly to the United States undetected.

The Amazon warrior pushes a button on the Invisible Jet's control panel to fire the engines. Then she pulls back on the control stick and zooms into the sky.

A short time later, Wonder Woman arrives in New York City. Up ahead, she sees a crowd of terrified people running down the street.

To her surprise, Wonder Woman spots Ares, the God of War, standing in the middle of a street. The Minotaur stands next to him.

The Amazon Princess quickly lands her jet, grabs her sword and shield, and jumps out of the cockpit.

Ares is Wonder Woman's most dangerous foe. The God of War feeds on the anger of others. He grows even stronger when those around him use violence.

Turn the page.

"So it was you who freed the Minotaur," says Wonder Woman.

"The Minotaur is just one of many challenges you may face today," Ares says with a harsh laugh. "Look behind you!"

Wonder Woman spins around and gasps.

Three flying monsters known as Harpies soar toward the city. And in New York Harbor, a towering waterspout suddenly erupts from the water.

"Land, air, or sea," says Ares. "You must choose, Amazon. The fate of New York City is in your hands."

If Wonder Woman confronts the Minotaur, turn to page 14.
If Wonder Woman flies up to confront the Harpies, turn to page 16.
If Wonder Woman flies to the waterspout, turn to page 19.

"You can't fool me with your distractions, Ares," says Wonder Woman. "I came here to return the Minotaur to Themyscira and place it back behind Doom's Doorway. And that's what I intend to do!"

The hero takes a step toward the Minotaur.

The massive creature towers over the Amazon. With a mighty roar, the Minotaur lunges toward Wonder Woman.

WHOOSH!

The Amazon soars into the air seconds before the Minotaur reaches her. She swings her sword and its flat side strikes the back of the Minotaur's head. The monster crashes to the ground with a loud thud.

The Minotaur quickly scrambles to its feet. It glares at Wonder Woman as she hovers nearby.

HA! HA! HA!

Ares laughs and rubs his hands together. He eagerly watches what will happen next.

Suddenly, the Minotaur turns around and reaches down. It grabs the top of a nearby fire hydrant with its two large hands and twists.

CRUNNNNCH!

The Minotaur easily rips the top off the fire hydrant. A rush of water sprays into the air. The street quickly floods.

Wonder Woman zooms into action. She pulls her glittering Amazonian shield from her back and flies over to the damaged fire hydrant.

BLAM!

Wonder Woman slams her shield down on the top of the gushing hydrant. The shield's impact fuses the metal hydrant closed again.

As the water drains into the gutters, the Amazon warrior looks up to see the Minotaur running down the street.

"Are you done playing in the water, Amazon?" Ares asks as he steps forward. "Are you ready to face the God of War himself?"

If Wonder Woman flies after the Minotaur, turn to page 22.
If Wonder Woman confronts Ares, turn to page 29.

"Very clever, Ares," says Wonder Woman. "But there is no way I'm going to let those Harpies tear this city to shreds."

Harpies are terrifying monsters with female faces and vulture bodies. They have long feathered wings and dangerously sharp claws. Their evil faces smile with delight as they see Wonder Woman standing below them. Harpies love nothing more than to torment Amazons.

SCREECH! SCREECH!

The Harpies's screams fill the air. They flap their wings and flex their razor-sharp claws.

WHOOSH!

Wonder Woman zooms into the sky. She heads directly toward the three flying creatures.

They quickly veer away from the Amazon and fly toward New York's skyscrapers. Wonder Woman knows that she has to stop them before they reach the city's buildings.

The Harpies move fast, but Wonder Woman moves faster. She draws closer to the creatures.

Wonder Woman draws back her arm and swings it through the air.

BLAM! She slams her fist against one of the Harpies.

The Harpy screams in pain and is knocked off balance. The creature tumbles through the air.

The other two creatures swoop down to catch the falling Harpy. Then they continue flying toward the city.

ZOOOM! Suddenly, the sound of a nearby passenger jet fills the air. The Harpies look up at the jet as it flies above them. Their mouths open wide in evil grins.

SCREEECH!

The Harpies soar skyward, heading directly toward the jet.

Wonder Woman zooms after them.

The Harpies land on the wing of the jet. The creatures screech joyfully as their sharp talons scratch the wing's smooth metal surface.

Turn the page.

Wonder Woman lands on the end of the wing, just steps away from the Harpies.

Startled passengers inside the jet look out their windows and scream with fright at the sight before them.

Wonder Woman draws in her breath, expanding her lungs as much as possible.

SWOOOOSH!

The Amazon exhales and blows the startled Harpies off the side of the wing. They tumble through the air.

Wonder Woman jumps off the wing in pursuit. The jet safely flies away.

The Harpies quickly recover in midair. They flap their wings and hover, glaring at Wonder Woman. The creatures look undecided about what to do next.

If the Harpies attack Wonder Woman, turn to page 25.
If the Harpies fly toward the city, turn to page 31.

"Your evil knows no bounds, Ares," says Wonder Woman. "That waterspout will flood the city if left unchecked!"

Wonder Woman launches into the air and soars over New York Harbor. The gigantic waterspout pulls water from the surface of the harbor and shoots it hundreds of feet into the air. As the funnel spins faster and faster, it grows taller and taller.

Wonder Woman flies close to the tower of spiraling water.

"Ares has outdone himself this time," Wonder Woman says to herself. "It will take more than strength alone to tame this monstrous menace."

The hero starts to unfurl the golden lasso at her side.

Suddenly, a giant wave shoots out of the waterspout. The wave is shaped like a massive arm. It slams against Wonder Woman and knocks her backward.

Turn the page.

Wonder Woman falls into the harbor and sinks deep into the water. The wave forms a giant watery hand and wraps its wet fingers around the Amazon. She struggles to free herself as the massive hand squeezes her waist tighter and tighter. The hero reaches down to pry the fingers apart, but the watery hand holds firm.

Suddenly, the Amazon has an idea. She raises both arms high and then slams the two silver bracelets on her wrists together.

BLAM!

A massive explosion rocks the water, and a bright blast of energy shoots out of Wonder Woman's bracelets.

The blast forces the watery fingers to fly apart. Wonder Woman swims free.

Within seconds, the arm-shaped wave shrivels and disappears.

Wonder Woman zooms out of the harbor and flies back to the spinning waterspout.

It's getting even bigger, she thinks to herself.

TOOT! TOOT! A nearby tour boat honks its horn. The boat rocks in the dangerously high waves created by the waterspout.

"Help! Help!" cries a crowd of frightened people on the boat. They are being knocked around and thrown to the deck as the boat rocks up and down on the waves.

Wonder Woman knows she must make a quick decision.

If Wonder Woman dives into the water, turn to page 27.
If Wonder Woman flies to the tour boat, turn to page 33.

Wonder Woman flies down the street to take on the Minotaur.

I must stop this monster before he can do any more damage to the city, she thinks.

The creature stands in the middle of the road, blocking oncoming traffic. As it snorts with anger, puffs of gray smoke shoot out of its nostrils. Then it raises its muscled arms wide and reaches for a car heading straight toward it. The car skids to a stop directly in front of the monster.

EEK! HELP! HELP!

The frightened people inside the car cry out in fear.

BWA HA HA HA!

The Minotaur's harsh laugh echoes off the buildings. Then it easily lifts the car off the ground. The people inside brace themselves as the Minotaur shakes the vehicle over its head. The monster's massive hands dig into the car, crunching the vehicle's metal surface.

WHOOSH!

Wonder Woman zooms in, unfurling the golden lasso at her side. She quickly spins the rope in circles and creates a giant loop. Then she throws it around the car and pulls the lasso tightly around the vehicle.

With a mighty tug, Wonder Woman uses her incredible strength to yank the vehicle out of the Minotaur's hands and into her own. Then she carries the car farther down the street and gently sets it down on the ground.

"Thank you, Wonder Woman!" the relieved passengers call out to the hero.

Wonder Woman waves to them and then turns to face the Minotaur. The monster snorts with frustration and narrows its eyes at the Amazon.

If the Minotaur runs away, turn to page 35.
If the Minotaur attacks Wonder Woman, turn to page 52.

SCREEECH!

The Harpies flap their giant wings and dive through the air toward Wonder Woman. Their pointy claws glint in the sunlight, and their red eyes gleam with anger.

Within seconds, the Harpies surround Wonder Woman. The creatures slash their talons at her. They open their mouths wide and try to bite her with their sharp fangs.

"Get away from me, you foul beasts!" shouts Wonder Woman.

The Amazon whips her left hand to her side. As her fingers begin to close on the golden lasso at her hip, one of the Harpies sees what the hero is doing.

The Harpy lunges forward and grasps Wonder Woman's left arm within its mouth.

Wonder Woman gasps with pain as the Harpy's fangs lock onto her arm. The hero struggles to free her left arm, but the Harpy holds on tightly.

Turn the page.

With an evil chuckle, the Harpy shakes its head from side to side, flinging Wonder Woman through the air like a rag doll.

The other two Harpies screech with delight and open their mouths wide as they fly closer to Wonder Woman. Their pointy yellow fangs drip with saliva.

The pain in Wonder Woman's arm is overwhelming. She starts to lose consciousness.

SNAP! SNAP!

The other two Harpies reach out to bite Wonder Woman with their razor-sharp teeth. Their hot, stinking breath momentarily jolts the Amazon awake.

The Amazon swings her free arm through the air. The other two Harpies jump back to avoid Wonder Woman's powerful fist.

"Must stay awake . . . ," moans Wonder Woman as she fights to keep her eyes open.

If Wonder Woman is knocked unconscious, turn to page 38.

If Wonder Woman stays awake to battle the Harpies, turn to page 56.

SPLASH!

Wonder Woman dives into the water. The ice-cold ocean shocks her body for an instant. Then she kicks to the surface and uses powerful strokes to swim toward the rapidly growing waterspout. As she draws closer to the swirling water, she realizes she is not alone.

Aquaman, the golden-haired super hero, bobs in the choppy waves next to the swirling waterspout. One of Wonder Woman's closest friends, Aquaman is the King of the Seven Seas and can breathe underwater. He can also speak with all marine life.

Aquaman swims around the waterspout, studying it closely.

"What are you doing here?" asks Wonder Woman.

"I received an urgent call from the underwater creatures of New York Harbor," he replies. "This mysterious waterspout is upsetting their environment. What can you tell me about it?"

Turn the page.

"This waterspout is the work of Ares, the God of War," explains Wonder Woman.

"I haven't had a lot of experience dealing with Greek gods," Aquaman admits with a frown.

"*I* have," replies Wonder Woman. "Ares thrives on chaos and war, and he always has a lot of tricks up his—"

"Diana, look over there!" Aquaman exclaims, pointing behind Wonder Woman.

Wonder Woman spins around, and her jaw drops in dismay. A massive oil tanker floating near them suddenly tilts dangerously to one side. She knows it will be a disaster if the tanker sinks and spills oil into the harbor.

Wonder Woman turns back to Aquaman.

"Between the waterspout and that oil tanker, this situation is getting out of hand. We've got to act fast!" she says.

"Lead the way," Aquaman replies. "I'm right behind you."

If Wonder Woman deals with the waterspout, turn to page 40.
If Wonder Woman swims to the oil tanker, turn to page 59.

Ares looms over Wonder Woman. He spreads his arms wide.

"Submit to the God of War now and forever, Amazon," he says in a deep, booming voice.

Wonder Woman plants her feet on the ground and glares at the villain. Her hand touches the lasso at her side.

"Never, Ares," she replies.

"Very well, you have made your choice," he replies with disgust as his eyes begin to glow red.

ZAAAAP! Searing hot lasers shoot out of his eyes. The deadly rays head straight toward Wonder Woman.

The Amazon quickly lifts her arms and crosses her wrists in front of her face. The lasers slam into her silver bracelets.

WHAM! Wonder Woman skids backward as the deadly beams bounce off her bracelets and strike a nearby building. A dozen bricks tumble harmlessly to the ground.

Turn the page.

"Your bracelets may have saved you, Amazon," Ares says. "But can they save them?" The God of War points to a group of people gathered across the street. They huddle in the doorway of a building for safety.

Ares lifts his head and his eyes glow red once again. Wonder Woman leaps between the villain and the crowd, positioning herself to protect them from his laser blasts.

"Foolish Amazon," Ares says with a laugh. "I have more than one trick up my sleeve."

KER-BLAM! A deafening sound fills the air behind Wonder Woman. She spins around and her heart sinks.

At the far end of the street, a massive creature crashes through the pavement and crawls out of a gaping hole. The towering one-eyed monster beats its chest and stomps its feet.

"Choose, Amazon," taunts Ares. "Save those innocent bystanders or deal with the Cyclops!"

If Wonder Woman flies toward the crowd, turn to page 70.
If Wonder Woman flies toward the Cyclops, turn to page 86.

The Harpies shriek with delight as they zoom high above the skyscrapers of New York City. Wonder Woman is not far behind them.

The Harpies land on the roof of a building and glare at the Amazon warrior. They spread their wings wide and flex their dangerous claws, daring Wonder Woman to approach them.

Thinking fast, Wonder Woman pulls the shiny gold tiara from atop her head. She cocks her arm and flings the headgear toward the Harpies.

BLAM! BLAM! BLAM!

Her tiara bounces from one Harpy's head to another like a boomerang. The three creatures topple over onto the rooftop, knocked out.

Wonder Woman barely has time to collect her tiara before she hears a loud noise on the street below her. She looks over the edge of the roof, and her heart sinks.

Ares stands on the sidewalk below, but he is rapidly growing in size. He is now taller than some of the nearby buildings!

Turn the page.

The giant God of War laughs harshly as his eyes draw level with Wonder Woman. He glares at the Amazon.

"You think that your challenges are over because you defeated three birds?" the villain roars. "Your troubles are just beginning!"

"No, Ares. Your reign of terror is about to end!" declares Wonder Woman.

Ares continues to grow. He now towers over the building Wonder Woman stands on. He glances down at her and raises his arm high. He clenches his fist.

"What do you think, Amazon?" Ares says. "Do I destroy one of these buildings, or do I destroy you?"

The God of War smiles as he decides what to do next.

If Ares decides to destroy a building, turn to page 73.
If Ares decides to attack Wonder Woman, turn to page 89.

Wonder Woman flies over to the tour boat and cups her hands to her mouth.

"Hold on tight," she calls out to the frightened passengers. "I'm going to give you a lift."

Then the hero dives into the water and swims under the boat's hull. She positions herself directly underneath the vessel and extends her arms. She then kicks her legs and uses all of her amazing strength to lift the boat out of the water.

Seconds later she flies above the harbor, holding the boat aloft. She carries it to the nearby shore and sets it gently on the beach.

HOORAY! The passengers on the boat cheer and call out their thanks to Wonder Woman.

The Amazon zooms high above the harbor. She watches with relief as the waterspout melts into the waves.

Just then, blaring car horns and screams of terror cut through the air.

Wonder Woman's heart sinks. *What now?* she thinks.

Turn the page.

HONK! HONK!

Following the sound of the car horns, Wonder Woman spots the massive Brooklyn Bridge connecting Manhattan to Brooklyn. Her eyes track across the cars stopped on the bridge deck and go up one of the bridge's two tall stone towers. A giant, multi-colored dragon stands on top of the tower. The creature extends its ribbed wings and flaps them in the air.

EEEK! EEEK!

Wonder Woman then turns in the direction of the screams. They rise up from the tourists standing at the base of the Statue of Liberty on Liberty Island.

On a normal day, the tourists would be enjoying the views of the historic statue. But not today. The tourists scream and run away from the island's edge. They flee from a multi-headed monster that emerges from the harbor and crawls onto the island.

If Wonder Woman flies to the Brooklyn Bridge, turn to page 75.
If Wonder Woman flies to Liberty Island, turn to page 92.

The Minotaur dashes down the street.

BLAM! CRASH! SMASH!

Along the way it slams its giant fists into parked cars, mailboxes, and light poles.

A block and a half away, the monster pauses to look back at Wonder Woman. It then turns and ducks into a nearby alley.

"Now I've got you," Wonder Woman says to herself. "That alley is a dead end."

The Amazon flies toward the alley. She lands on the sidewalk to corner the monster.

But the Minotaur lunges out of the alley with blinding speed. It kicks its leg.

WHAM! The monster's foot crashes against Wonder Woman. The Amazon topples to the ground and lands on her back.

CRUNCH! CRUNCH! CRUNCH!

The Minotaur savagely pulls bricks out of a nearby building. It soon has a half-dozen of them gathered in its giant hands.

Turn to page 37.

Wonder Woman tries to get up, but the Minotaur is too fast for her. The creature cocks an arm and uses all its strength to hurl a brick at Wonder Woman. Then it throws another. And another.

Wonder Woman quickly rolls to one side. The bricks land on the sidewalk and explode into clouds of dust.

The Minotaur gathers more bricks in its hands. As it does so, Wonder Woman jumps to her feet.

The Amazon quickly crosses her arms in front of her face. The silver bracelets on her wrists glint in the sunlight.

BLAM! BLAM! BLAM!

The bricks bounce off her bracelets and ricochet back toward the Minotaur. The impact of the flying bricks knocks the creature to the ground. The Minotaur howls in anger.

Turn to page 42.

The Harpy holds the Amazon's left arm tightly within its mouth. Then it bites down hard.

CRUNCH! Shooting pain courses through Wonder Woman's arm. The hero loses consciousness and her body goes limp.

The Harpies cackle with delight. They fly high above the city streets, screeching triumphantly. People below look up in horror at the sight of Wonder Woman hanging limply from the mouth of one of the foul creatures.

The Harpies zoom back to the harbor, still carrying the Amazon. They soar high above the water, and then the Harpy holding Wonder Woman opens its mouth. The unconscious Amazon tumbles toward the water.

SPLASH! Wonder Woman lands in the harbor and sinks beneath its frigid surface.

The Harpies flap their massive wings and shriek with joy.

Wonder Woman slowly sinks deeper into the harbor.

Suddenly, her eyelids start to flutter. The icy cold water jolts her awake. Her fingers start to twitch. She looks down at her left arm. The bite marks left by the Harpy have already started to heal.

I need a plan to finish off those Harpies once and for all, Wonder Woman thinks.

Without even a thought, her right hand moves closer to the lasso coiled at her side.

That's it! she thinks.

The Amazon warrior grasps the lasso in her hand. With a quick movement, she unfurls it. Even in the darkness of the harbor waters, her lasso gives off a golden glow.

Wonder Woman kicks her legs and swims toward the surface. She moves faster and faster.

SPLASH! The hero zooms out of the water, her lasso coiled in her right hand.

Turn to page 45.

Wonder Woman turns to face Aquaman.

"We've got to take down this waterspout," she declares. "Before we do, you better tell your ocean friends to steer clear."

Aquaman closes his eyes and concentrates. After a few seconds, he opens them and turns to Wonder Woman. He looks worried.

"I tried to warn the marine life here to swim away from the harbor," he says. "But something blocked my ability to talk to them."

"It must be Ares," says Wonder Woman. "I need to disrupt his powers."

She pauses to study the swirling water. "Perhaps the key to defeating this waterspout is not at its base, but near its top," she says.

She removes the golden lasso at her side and flies to the top of the waterspout.

The dangerous column of swirling water now rises higher than some of the skyscrapers in the nearby city. It churns up the surface of the harbor as it slowly inches closer to the shore.

If this funnel gets too close to the city, it's going to hit the shore like a typhoon, thinks Wonder Woman. *I have to stop it now.*

The Amazon warrior twirls her lasso, making a wider and wider loop.

"If I can just get my lasso around the waterspout, maybe I can drag it farther out into the harbor," she calls out to Aquaman.

But before the hero can fling her lasso, the waterspout suddenly turns around.

BLAM!

It slams into Wonder Woman and knocks the Amazon unconscious. The lasso slips from her hand as she splashes into the water. Then she slowly sinks to the bottom of the harbor.

Turn to page 48.

"Arrrrgh!" bellows the angry Minotaur as it lunges for Wonder Woman. The Amazon sidesteps the monster's attack and reaches for the top of her head. She grasps the shiny gold tiara that she wears in her hair. Normally, Wonder Woman wears the tiara to show that she is the royal princess of Themyscira. But today her headgear serves another purpose.

With a flick of her wrist, Wonder Woman flings the tiara at the Minotaur.

ZING!

In times of need, the Amazon Princess's golden tiara doubles as a razor-sharp weapon. It slices through the air, heading straight for the monster.

The Minotaur's eyes widen with surprise. And then it smiles. As the tiara zooms closer, the monster opens its mouth wide. Massive fangs as sharp as swords line its jaws.

CHOMP! The Minotaur catches Wonder Woman's tiara with its massive mouth. It bites down hard on the flying weapon.

CRUNCH! The sound of grinding metal fills the air. The Minotaur spits the cracked tiara out of its mouth. It clatters to the ground.

Wonder Woman quickly removes her sword from its sheath on her back. She grasps the weapon in her right hand and extends it menacingly toward the Minotaur.

"I *will* defeat you, monster!" she calls out bravely.

BOOM! With a clap of thunder, Ares suddenly appears behind Wonder Woman. Before she can turn around, his eyes glow red.

ZAAAAAAP!

The God of War blasts deadly lasers from his eyes. The bright red beams strike Wonder Woman's back.

Wonder Woman groans in pain and falls to the ground. Her sword tumbles from her hand and lands in the street. The Amazon slowly loses consciousness.

Turn the page.

The Minotaur smiles and steps forward. Its mouth opens wider, displaying dozens of pointed fangs. The monster leans over Wonder Woman. It has a hungry look on its face.

"Stop!" commands Ares.

The Minotaur looks up in confusion.

"She is no threat to us now," says Ares. "I have other plans for you."

Ares grabs the Minotaur and harshly shoves the creature down the street.

"I have a city to conquer," says the God of War. "And after that, a country. And after that . . . a whole world!"

Ares takes a final look at the fallen Amazon and then walks away.

BWA HA HA HA HA! His laughter echoes throughout the city streets.

THE END

To follow another path, turn to page 12.

Wonder Woman soars high above the harbor, but there is no sign of the three Harpies. She zooms toward the city, flying high above the skyscrapers. Suddenly, she sees the Harpies, flying in close formation near City Hall.

Birds of a feather flock together, thinks Wonder Woman. *Which gives me an idea.*

The hero heads straight toward the Harpies.

SCREECH! The creatures scream in anger when they see that the Amazon has survived.

Wonder Woman swings her lasso, creating a giant loop.

Just as she is about to grab the Harpies with her lasso, the creatures fly in three separate directions. They cackle with delight as they avoid Wonder Woman's trap.

Then one Harpy turns and dives toward Wonder Woman. It tries to grab the golden lasso with its claws. The hero swings her arm around and smashes her fist against the Harpy's feathered body.

Turn the page.

The injured Harpy screams in pain as it somersaults backward. Wonder Woman reaches out and grabs the Harpy's feet.

"How about taking a little spin?" she says to the angry creature.

Wonder Woman spins the creature around in circles, faster and faster. The Harpy flaps its wings and protests loudly, but Wonder Woman holds the creature tightly.

After a minute of frenzied spinning, Wonder Woman releases the dizzy creature. It tumbles through the air and slams into the other two Harpies.

SCREECH! SCREECH!

The Harpies scream with anger as they bump up against each other. Their wings tangle together, and they quickly fall toward the ground. They look like a giant ball of feathers and claws and angry gnashing teeth.

Wonder Woman knows she has to move fast.

The hero once again spins her lasso to create a giant circle. With a mighty flick, she throws the rope and loops it around the three angry Harpies.

The Amazon warrior tugs on the lasso with all of her strength. It tightens around the three creatures. They struggle and screech, but Wonder Woman's lasso holds them in place.

"You can struggle all you want," Wonder Woman says to the furious Harpies. "But there will be no escape for you now."

The three creatures grow quiet and glare at Wonder Woman. They know what the future holds for them.

Soon they will once again be trapped behind Doom's Doorway.

THE END

To follow another path, turn to page 12.

"Diana! Diana! Can you hear me?" Aquaman asks as he leans over his friend. Wonder Woman lies at the bottom of the harbor. Her eyes are closed, and she is not moving.

Aquaman spies the glowing golden lasso draped over a sunken barge on the harbor floor. He quickly swims over and retrieves it.

"I don't know if this will make any difference, but here's your lasso," Aquaman says. He carefully places the rope in her hand and closes her fingers around it.

Suddenly, Wonder Woman's eyes pop open. She smiles at Aquaman and then zooms to the surface.

SPLASH!

Seconds later, Wonder Woman once again soars high above the rapidly swirling tempest of water.

"I think I know just how to deal with this waterspout," she calls down to Aquaman.

Turn to page 50.

The waterspout now rises 300 feet above the harbor. Like a lumbering giant, it edges dangerously close to the city's shoreline.

Wonder Woman quickly unloops her lasso.

"How do I stop a waterspout that is spinning clockwise?" Wonder Woman asks herself. "Simple! I surround it from top to bottom with my lasso spinning counter-clockwise!"

Wonder Woman twirls her lasso around the waterspout. The rope magically extends until it coils around the entire tower of water. Wonder Woman then spins the lasso counter-clockwise.

WHOOSH! WHOOSH! WHOOSH!

The force of the spinning waterspout nearly pulls the lasso out of Wonder Woman's hands, but she holds on tight. Her muscles strain as she twirls the lasso faster.

Ever so slowly, the speed of the rotating waterspout lessens.

Wonder Woman spins the lasso even faster. The waterspout begins to shrink.

Soon, the waterspout shrivels to barely a trickle of water bubbling in the harbor. Wonder Woman gathers up her lasso.

"Nice job, Diana!" Aquaman says as he happily waves to her.

"I'm able to talk to the marine life in the harbor again," he says. "You've broken the God of War's spell!"

Wonder Woman smiles at her friend, but it's a sad smile.

"I'm glad to hear that everything is back to normal in the harbor," she says to her friend. "Unfortunately, though, Ares has an unlimited number of evil plans and spells. I'm afraid my work here is not done."

Minutes later, the hero flies high above the skyscrapers of New York City. Ares will never rest. And neither will Wonder Woman.

THE END

To follow another path, turn to page 12.

The Minotaur takes a step forward and draws back its giant fist. Wonder Woman tries to jump out of the way, but the Minotaur is too fast. Its fist strikes Wonder Woman square in the jaw.

WHACK!

The Amazon stumbles backward. The Minotaur swings its other fist to strike her again. This time Wonder Woman ducks out of the way.

The Amazon warrior plants her feet and sets herself for the Minotaur's next blow. As the monster swings again, Wonder Woman crosses her wrists in front of her face. Her silver bracelets block the blow.

CLANG!

The Minotaur bellows in pain. It staggers backward, rubbing its throbbing fist with its other hand.

Wonder Woman clenches her bruised jaw in anger. She leaps forward to strike the Minotaur.

The Minotaur is ready for Wonder Woman's attack. It opens its arms wide and wraps them around the Amazon. Locked in battle, the two opponents crash into a nearby store front, shattering its display window.

Still wrestling, they trip over a low stone bench on the sidewalk. As they both tumble head over heels, the back of the Minotaur's head smacks the sidewalk. The creature winces with pain. Its face fills with overwhelming rage.

ROAR!

With a fearsome growl, the Minotaur stretches to bite Wonder Woman's arm. Its sharp fangs drip with saliva.

The alarmed Amazon flexes her muscles, breaking the Minotaur's hold. She quickly pulls her arm out of harm's way.

Wonder Woman jumps to her feet and soars into the air. The Minotaur narrows its eyes in anger.

Turn the page.

Wonder Woman zooms down the block and turns around. She then flies at lightning-fast speed straight toward the Minotaur.

The creature smiles at Wonder Woman with evil delight. It stretches its muscled arms wide to catch the Amazon.

"Sorry, big guy," Wonder Woman says. "But that's not going to work this time."

ZOOM! ZOOM! ZOOM!

Wonder Woman circles the creature just beyond its reach. The Minotaur spins and grasps at empty air as she loops faster and faster. Soon the Minotaur grows dizzy.

"What's the matter? Can't you catch me?" calls out Wonder Woman.

The Minotaur staggers on its feet, dazed and confused. All it can see is a red, blue, and gold blur as Wonder Woman accelerates her speedy loops.

Turn to page 62.

The Harpy bites down harder on Wonder Woman's arm. The Amazon groans softly. Her eyes begin to close. The other Harpies shriek with delight.

SCREECH! SCREECH!

The shrill pitch of their voices pierces the air, and Wonder Woman's eyes snap open. She tries to pull her arm free, but the Harpy holds it tightly within its mouth.

Using all of her strength, Wonder Woman thrusts her legs forward. Her feet slam against the chest of the Harpy locked onto her arm. The powerful kick knocks the wind out of the foul beast and forces it to open its mouth. Released from the Harpy's grip, Wonder Woman pulls away from the creature.

The three Harpies flap their wings and shriek angrily.

As Wonder Woman rubs the pain out of her arm, the vile creatures peel away and swoop toward the concrete jungle of New York City. In an instant, Wonder Woman zooms after them.

The Harpies soar between the city's tallest skyscrapers. Suddenly, one Harpy banks to the right and its wing slices through a building's windows.

CRASH! Shards of broken glass tumble toward the ground.

Wonder Woman looks down and spots a crowd of people looking up in fear. *If I don't act fast, that falling glass is sure to injure someone,* Wonder Woman thinks.

Wonder Woman abandons her pursuit of the Harpies and dives after the glass. Quickly and carefully, she collects each piece before it hits the ground.

Meanwhile, the Harpies land on top of a tall building and look around to see what kind of trouble they can cause.

"I need a plan," Wonder Woman says to herself. "Somehow I have to stop these creatures before they put any more people in danger."

Suddenly, an idea pops into her head.

Turn the page.

Wonder Woman lands on the roof and faces the Harpies. The creatures hiss and spread their wings. They start to lurch toward her. Wonder Woman stands her ground.

I have to let them get close enough to see the expression on my face, thinks Wonder Woman. *I need to make them think that I'm afraid of them.*

Just before the Harpies reach her, Wonder Woman backs away. She makes her face look afraid. She raises her eyebrows and makes her eyes grow wide.

The Harpies watch with surprise as the Amazon moves slowly to the edge of the roof. The hero looks behind her, pauses for a moment, and then dives off the roof.

SCREECH! SCREECH!

The Harpies scream with delight as their foe disappears from sight. The mighty Amazon is a coward!

Turn to page 65.

As the swirling waterspout churns up the harbor, the oil tanker tilts dangerously from side to side. Water crashes onto the ship's deck and the crew calls out for help as waves batter the tanker.

Wonder Woman soars toward the vessel. One sailor slips and falls on the water-drenched deck. He slides to one side of the tanker and then tumbles over the railing.

"Man overboard!" the captain yells.

Wonder Woman zooms into action and dives into the harbor. She grabs the sailor's hand and pulls him out of the water.

WHAM!

Just as the hero sets the sailor down safely on the deck, a towering wave slams against the ship. The oil tanker starts to sink.

Wonder Woman realizes she only has seconds to save the crew.

"Gather together on the deck," she calls down to the sailors. "I'll carry you to safety."

Turn the page.

SWOOSH! SWOOSH!

Wonder Woman swirls her golden lasso into a giant loop. She soars above the oil tanker and tosses the rope around the crew. With a quick tug, the golden lasso gathers up the sailors.

As the oil tanker sinks, Wonder Woman lifts the sailors to safety. She tows them to the nearby shore and sets them on the rocky beach.

Before the sailors have time to thank her, Wonder Woman dives back into the harbor.

SPLASH!

Like a speeding torpedo, the Amazon warrior swims toward the sinking ship. She knows the tanker will cause an environmental disaster if it leaks oil into the harbor.

As the ship slips beneath the waves, Wonder Woman spots Aquaman bobbing on the surface. The two dive underwater and swim as fast as they can. They soon reach the tanker, which now settles on the floor of the harbor.

Both heroes gasp in horror.

A steady flow of black oil gushes out of a huge gash on the bottom of the tanker.

Wonder Woman and Aquaman grasp the back of the giant tanker. Using all of their might, they lift the ship off the harbor floor. Then they push the vessel to the surface.

"Thanks, Aquaman," Wonder Woman says. "I'll take it from here."

With a final burst of power, the Amazon hoists the tanker out of the water and carries it to shore.

Turn to page 67.

The Minotaur wobbles dizzily on its feet.

Suddenly, Wonder Woman pauses in midair and draws back her fist.

BLAM!

The Amazon warrior punches the Minotaur so hard that it topples to the ground. The creature moans and closes its eyes. The Minotaur may be knocked out, but Wonder Woman knows it won't stay that way for long.

As the hero struggles to catch her breath, Ares steps out of the shadows.

"Well done, Amazon," he says, clapping his hands. "Now you need to finish the job. Take your sword and strike down the Minotaur!"

Wonder Woman looks at Ares, and then she stares at the Minotaur. The monster will soon awaken and once again threaten the city.

She reaches back and places a hand on the hilt of her sword. Ares watches carefully as Wonder Woman removes her sword from its sheath on her back.

"Yes, do it now," the God of War urges her. "The Minotaur has killed many brave warriors. It deserves to meet its doom."

Wonder Woman hears the God of War's words. Anger stirs deep within her. She could avenge the deaths of many fallen warriors with just one stroke. She raises her sword above the unconscious Minotaur's head.

"It won't feel a thing," whispers Ares.

But as Wonder Woman stares at the Minotaur's face, a memory flashes in her mind. She remembers a promise she made to her mother long ago. When she was just a little girl on the island of Themyscira, Diana pledged to control her mighty powers and always show her foes mercy.

"No, Ares," says Wonder Woman as she lowers her sword. "Your anger will not infect me. I will not take the Minotaur's life."

Wonder Woman returns her weapon to its sheath and unhooks her golden lasso.

Turn the page.

"I will return the creature to Themyscira and once again place it behind Doom's Doorway," the hero says.

The God of War's face fills with rage.

"You are a fool!" he bellows. "The day will come when you and your fellow Amazons will learn that anger is more powerful than mercy!"

POOF!

Ares disappears in a thick cloud of smoke.

Wonder Woman smiles as she binds the Minotaur with her lasso.

"Ares is wrong," she says to herself. "That day will *never* come!"

THE END

To follow another path, turn to page 12.

As the Harpies cackle with delight on top of the building, Wonder Woman zooms away. Wasting no time, she flies back to the street where her Invisible Jet is parked.

Seeing no sign of Ares, the Amazon warrior quickly climbs into the cockpit of her amazing vehicle. As soon as she closes the cockpit canopy, she instantly turns invisible herself.

WHOOSH! Wonder Woman pilots her jet high above the skyscrapers of New York City, unseen by all. She heads straight back to the rooftop where the Harpies now roost.

When the hero reaches the building, she silently hovers the jet above their heads. The Harpies have no idea she lingers nearby.

We'll see if a surprise attack can defeat these three creatures, thinks Wonder Woman.

In one fluid motion, the Amazon warrior springs her trap. She pulls her sword from its sheath, opens the cockpit canopy, and leaps from the Invisible Jet.

Turn the page.

The Harpies blink in surprise as Wonder Woman suddenly lands before them with a **THUD!**

They shriek with anger as Wonder Woman twirls her glittering sword in the bright sunlight.

SNIP! SNIP! SNIP!

Wonder Woman's blade clips the wing feathers from the Harpies. Without those feathers, the Harpies can no longer fly. They stumble around on the roof, bumping into one another.

Wonder Woman quickly grabs her lasso and tosses it around the creatures. The Harpies hiss and scream, but they are unable to move.

"The sooner you three angry birds are locked up in a cage behind Doom's Doorway, the better," Wonder Woman says with a smile. Then she leads the terrible trio to her Invisible Jet.

THE END

To follow another path, turn to page 12.

Wonder Woman stands beside the ship on the rocky beach. She breathes heavily from the strain of lifting the heavy tanker. Aquaman floats in the water nearby.

"Nice job, Diana!" he calls out.

"Thanks, but there's no time to rest," she replies. "I think I know how we can clean up the oil. First, I'm going to need my Invisible Jet."

"Your Invisible Jet?" says Aquaman. "But I won't be able to see you. How will I know when to help you?"

"Don't worry," she says. "You'll know!"

Wonder Woman turns and runs through the streets of New York City. When she reaches her Invisible Jet, she hops into the cockpit and takes off. The jet soars high above the harbor.

SPLASH! The Invisible Jet nosedives into the water and zooms toward the mass of oil rising toward the surface. As Wonder Woman guides her plane closer, she sees Aquaman frantically moving fish out of harm's way.

Turn the page.

I don't know if this is going to work, Wonder Woman thinks, *but it's worth a try!*

WHOOSH! WHOOSH! WHOOSH!

Wonder Woman pilots the Invisible Jet in circles around the oil spill. The jet swirls through the water, faster and faster. Soon the oil spins into a swirling black whirlpool.

Now, Aquaman! the Amazon thinks.

Almost as if he could read her mind, Aquaman knows it's his time to act.

BLAM!

He pounds his golden trident on the harbor floor. The impact creates a giant wave that carries the swirling oil to the surface.

Aquaman follows the wave and commands it to head directly toward the beached oil tanker.

WHOOSH! With a wave of his trident, Aquaman forces the oil-filled wave high into the air. He then maneuvers the sludgy mass directly into the tanker's large storage container.

As the last drop of oil falls into the container, Aquaman turns to find Wonder Woman at his side. He breathes a sigh of relief, and Wonder Woman smiles.

Just then, a harsh laugh spills from the depths of the city and echoes across the harbor.

"It's Ares!" the Amazon says quietly. "One challenge down. But there's no telling how many more he has planned."

THE END

To follow another path, turn to page 12.

Wonder Woman knows the safety of the innocent people behind her comes first. She positions herself between them and Ares.

"So, Amazon, do you think those people appreciate your help?" Ares says with a chuckle.

SWISH! A brick flies through the air and almost hits Wonder Woman's shoulder. Another brick whizzes past her ear. Then four more bricks crash at her feet.

The Amazon turns around, and her mouth drops open in surprise. The people gathered across the street are throwing bricks at her!

"Who asked Wonder Woman to help us?" yells an elderly man as he gets ready to throw another brick.

"Yeah!" agrees a woman wearing a nurse's uniform. "We don't need super heroes wrecking our city."

"Those laser beams you deflected just damaged my apartment building!" screams another woman.

Turn to page 72.

Wonder Woman turns to face Ares.

"This is *your* doing, God of War!" she declares. "You are filling their minds with rage. You are making them turn against me."

Ares merely shrugs and slowly disappears into the shadows of a building behind him.

"Wonder Woman is a menace to society!" yells another man, stepping toward the Amazon. "She needs to be stopped!"

The people murmur in anger and move closer.

"I say we drive her away once and for all!" screams the elderly man.

The crowd grabs more bricks off the street and starts flinging them at Wonder Woman. The Amazon uses her silver bracelets to deflect them as she slowly backs away from the angry mob.

HA! HA! HA! Wonder Woman can hear Ares's harsh laughter behind her.

"Where is your grateful public now, Amazon?" he taunts.

Turn to page 77.

Ares swings one of his massive arms in a circle.

WHAM!

His fist crashes against the side of a nearby building. Windows shatter on the top floor, and bricks go flying through the air.

"Help! Help!" A voice cries out from behind a broken window.

Wonder Woman flies into action. She zooms over to the building and dives through the broken window. Seconds later she emerges carrying a very frightened woman.

Wonder Woman swoops down the outside of the building, holding the woman tightly. The Amazon uses her free hand to quickly gather up the falling bricks and shards of broken glass before they hit the ground.

Wonder Woman gently places the woman on the sidewalk.

The frazzled woman smiles. "I don't know how I can ever thank you," she says.

Turn the page.

Wonder Woman places a reassuring hand on the woman's shoulder.

"Don't worry about that right now," replies the Amazon. "Go inside the lobby of this building. You'll be safe in there."

Wonder Woman zooms back into the sky to face Ares again. The God of War has moved down the street. He now stands in front of a building that is still under construction. Tall steel beams extend up from the ground, and several concrete floors have been built within them.

Wonder Woman flies over the construction site. To her relief, she notices that it looks deserted.

At least there won't be any people in danger here, thinks Wonder Woman.

Ares suddenly looks up and stares intently at her.

Wonder Woman shudders. It's almost as if he knows what she is thinking.

Turn to page 79.

The dragon atop the Brooklyn Bridge opens its mouth and roars. The creature stretches its long neck and glares down at the cars that have skidded to a stop. The air is filled with panicked screams from their passengers.

Wonder Woman zooms high above the harbor and flies toward the bridge. As she draws closer, she recognizes the dragon. It is Ladon, one of the largest and most dangerous monsters from Doom's Doorway.

Ladon smiles menacingly at Wonder Woman as she soars high above the tower.

"Welcome, Amazon," says Ladon with a sneer. "Ares didn't tell me that I would be seeing you. Come closer so we can get to know each other a little better."

Wonder Woman lands on the tower next to the dragon.

"Our meeting will have to be a short one," she says. "You are going back behind Doom's Doorway."

Turn the page.

Ladon laughs harshly and whips its long tail in a wide circle. The sharp spikes on the tail's tip glint in the bright sunlight.

"Oh . . . I'm afraid I have other plans," the dragon replies.

BLAM! BLAM! The dragon's tail crashes against the bridge's stone tower. Large chunks of stone come loose and fall.

"Oh, dear," says Ladon with a smile, "How careless of me. And how unfortunate for those humans down below."

Wonder Woman zooms into action, quickly removing the golden lasso from her waist.

As she flies toward the bridge deck, she swings her lasso in a circle. She throws her rope around the falling debris and pulls hard on the end of the cord. The lasso tightens around the chunks of stone.

Wonder Woman swings the lasso away from the bridge and releases the stones into the river below.

Turn to page 82.

Wonder Woman unloops the golden lasso from her side and flings it into the shadows behind her. The lasso encircles the God of War.

Ares howls with a rage. Anyone trapped within the golden lasso must speak the truth.

"Tell them, Ares!" commands Wonder Woman. "Tell them that you have clouded their minds with hatred!"

"Yes, these mindless humans were under my control," he snarls. "I will remove the spell."

The people slowly back away from Wonder Woman. They blink their eyes with confusion. Several offer apologies to the Amazon Princess.

Wonder Woman turns back to face Ares. But he is gone. He has disappeared from within the bounds of her lasso in a puff of black smoke.

"He won't be gone for long," Wonder Woman says quietly to herself. "And I'll be ready for him when he returns!"

THE END

To follow another path, turn to page 12.

Ares reaches with his massive arms and pulls on one of the steel beams.

CRAAAAAACK!

The steel beam snaps at its base. The concrete floors crack and crumble. Chunks of concrete fall to the ground.

BLAM! BLAM! BLAM!

Ares easily lifts the giant steel beam in one hand. He holds it high in the air like he is balancing a spear.

"I know you Amazons enjoy athletic contests," the villain calls out to Wonder Woman. "You can watch as I throw this javelin toward that crowd!"

Wonder Woman turns to look down the long concrete canyon formed by the city's skyscrapers. At the far end of Manhattan she sees a crowd gathered. They are nervously watching the battle between her and Ares.

There's no time to clear the people from the street, she thinks.

Turn the page.

Ares laughs and draws back his giant arm.

WHOOSH!

The God of War launches the steel beam with all of his might. It arcs high into the air and heads straight for the frightened crowd.

Wonder Woman doesn't wait to see if Ares hits his mark. She zooms through the air and loosens the golden lasso at her side. She tosses the lasso so that it loops around a building on one side of the street. Then she loops it around a building on the other side of the street. Back and forth she flies from one side of the street to the other.

Wonder Woman finishes weaving her lasso just before Ares's weapon arrives. Her lasso now looks like a giant spider web that extends across the entire street.

BOING!

The flying steel beam bounces off Wonder Woman's lasso net and sails back in the opposite direction. It heads directly toward Ares.

The God of War doesn't let his reversal of fortune slow him down.

POOF!

Ares vanishes in a cloud of smoke seconds before the steel beam can crash into him.

HOORAY!

The crowd at the end of the long street erupts in cheers and applause. Many people call out their thanks to Wonder Woman.

The Amazon warrior smiles in gratitude, but she knows that this isn't the end of Ares. The God of War will be back.

And Wonder Woman will be ready to take him down when he returns.

THE END

To follow another path, turn to page 12.

Wonder Woman flies back to the tower to confront Ladon. She lands next to the dragon.

The creature is staring at the bridge's metal cables, which hold up the roadway. Ladon turns to look at Wonder Woman with an evil smile.

"Here are a few fun facts for you," says Ladon. "Did you know that this bridge has more than 14,000 miles of metal wire cables? Each cable is made of 19 separate strands, and each strand has 278 separate wires. That's a *lot* of wires holding up the road below us!"

"Why are you telling me this?" asks Wonder Woman.

"I hope you won't think I'm bragging," replies Ladon. "But I intend to melt every single one of those wires."

Ladon leans closer to the wire cables attached to the tower. The dragon opens its mouth wide, preparing to release a blast of flames.

Wonder Woman knows that a dragon's fire will easily melt the wires of the bridge.

I have to move fast, thinks Wonder Woman.

The Amazon jumps forward and unloops the golden lasso at her side. But Ladon is too fast for Wonder Woman.

SMASH!

The dragon whips its tail before Wonder Woman can swing her lasso. Ladon's tail crashes against the Amazon and knocks her off balance. Wonder Woman tumbles off the tower and falls toward the water below.

"Your rope tricks aren't going to work this time," says Ladon with a sneer. "This isn't my first rodeo!"

Wonder Woman quickly recovers in midair and soars high above the tower.

"Back again?" says Ladon with a sigh. "Very well. I'll deal with you before I melt these wires."

Wonder Woman flies closer to the dragon. She has an idea how to defeat Ladon.

Turn to page 85.

"I think you might need a backup plan," she says. "I doubt your flames are strong enough to melt these wire cables."

"Not strong enough?" shouts the dragon, glaring at the hero. "I'll show *you* their strength!"

Ladon opens its mouth and blasts Wonder Woman with red-hot flames.

ROAAAAR!

The Amazon quickly places her shield in front of her body. The flames strike it and bounce back at the dragon.

"Arrrrrgh!" screams Ladon as the flames crash against its body. The creature falls off the tower and disappears in the icy water below.

Wonder Woman sighs with relief.

"It looks like Ladon won't be burning any bridges today after all," she says. Then she leaps into the water to gather up the drenched dragon and take it back to Doom's Doorway.

THE END

To follow another path, turn to page 12.

I've got to stop the Cyclops before it destroys the city, Wonder Woman thinks.

The hero zooms between the city's skyscrapers and flies straight toward the one-eyed creature. The Cyclops is one of the largest and most savage monsters ever held behind Doom's Doorway. It was sent to that dark prison after it ate six sailors.

The giant creature towers over the street. The Cyclops flexes its arms, showing off its massive muscles. Its one eye blinks in the middle of its forehead. It tries to focus on the mighty Amazon flying directly toward it with her arms extended.

BLAM!

Wonder Woman's fists slam against the Cyclops's body. The hero falls to the ground, her hands aching from the impact of the blow.

The monster wobbles—temporarily knocked off balance—but it quickly recovers. The Cyclops clenches its jaw, and its breath hisses in and out between its teeth.

The Cyclops aims a wide swinging punch at Wonder Woman's head. The Amazon flinches away, quickly ducking and covering her head with her shield.

CLANG!

The Cyclops's giant hand bounces off Wonder Woman's shield. The monster roars in pain.

The Cyclops then reaches forward and grabs a parked city bus within its massive hands. Wonder Woman sees with relief that the bus is empty.

With barely a grunt, the monster lifts the bus off the ground.

The Cyclops holds the bus high above its head. It then launches the vehicle into the air. The bus heads straight toward Wonder Woman.

The Amazon quickly unfurls the golden lasso at her side. Within seconds, she twirls it into a giant loop.

"You want to play catch?" she calls out to the Cyclops. "Okay, catch *this!*"

Turn the page.

Wonder Woman loops her lasso around the flying bus and pulls it tight. She swings the bus in the air, around and around.

"Have you ever played with a yo-yo?" she calls out to the Cyclops.

The monster blinks its eye, confused.

"It works something like this," says Wonder Woman as she hurls the vehicle back at the surprised Cyclops.

WHAM!

The bus crashes into the monster. The Cyclops stumbles backward and slams into a nearby brick building.

The monster's eye slowly closes as the creature slumps to the ground.

Wonder Woman steps cautiously toward the monster. She withdraws her sword from its sheath on her back. She leans closer and feels the creature's hot breath on her face. Now that she knows the Cyclops is still alive, she considers her next move.

Turn to page 96.

BLAM!

Ares slams his fist on the rooftop on which Wonder Woman stands. Bricks and chunks of cement tumble down the side of the building.

Wonder Woman jumps off the edge of the roof and collects all the falling debris before it hits anyone on the sidewalk below.

As she places the debris on the ground, Wonder Woman pauses for a moment. *I have to get Ares away from the city sidewalks where people might get hurt,* she thinks.

The towering God of War stomps into view and reaches his giant hand to grab the Amazon.

Wonder Woman zooms through the air, heading toward the harbor.

"It is useless to flee, Amazon!" Ares bellows as he runs after her. "You will bow down to the God of War, or you will be destroyed!"

Wonder Woman soars over the harbor. Behind her, she can hear the giant God of War's heavy footsteps echoing in the city streets.

Turn the page.

ZOOOOM!

The mechanical roar of jets suddenly cuts across the sky.

Wonder Woman quickly looks up. Military fighter planes soar through the sky, flying toward Ares. She sees that each plane bristles with missiles pointed directly at the villain.

The God of War reaches the edge of the harbor and pauses to study the military planes. He chuckles.

"Do they really think these pitiful devices will harm the God of War?" he says with scorn.

Wonder Woman knows she has no time to spare. While Ares watches the incoming planes, she runs to her Invisible Jet.

Wonder Woman jumps into her jet's cockpit and instantly becomes invisible.

Distracted by the fighter planes, Ares doesn't notice that Wonder Woman has vanished. He also doesn't hear the silent engines of the Invisible Jet as it launches into the sky.

Wonder Woman guides her vehicle directly at the military planes. She knows that the pilots have no idea who they are dealing with and what he is capable of.

Ares will just swat the missiles out of the air with the back of his hand, thinks Wonder Woman. *He'll send those exploding missiles directly toward the city.*

Ares knows this as well, and he steps closer to the city buildings as the fighter planes zoom toward him.

"Fire away!" he yells with an evil laugh.

Turn to page 100.

Wonder Woman zooms across the harbor, heading for Liberty Island. As she flies over the Statue of Liberty, she sees that the massive creature has six heads. Wonder Woman instantly recognizes the monster as Scylla.

Scylla is a fearsome creature that lives in a cave near a narrow channel between Italy and Sicily. Scylla has an endless desire to eat. It loves nothing more than to gobble down sailors who venture too close to its home.

Scylla's six snake-like heads have glowing yellow eyes and dangerously sharp teeth. The heads swirl around on its six long necks, and it emits a low hissing sound as it crawls closer to the Statue of Liberty.

Fleeing in fear, the tourists on the island now huddle together inside the statue. Scylla sniffs the air, searching for the scent of humans.

Wonder Woman flies toward the creature. The Amazon takes care to keep her distance from Scylla's mouths, which open and close with horrible crunching noises.

Turn to page 94.

"Scylla, you have no reason to be here," calls out Wonder Woman. "I know that you have been brought forth by Ares. Move away from the statue, and I will offer you safe passage to Doom's Doorway."

Scylla extends one of its necks, lunging for Wonder Woman. The monster's giant mouth opens wide, dripping with foam.

SNAP!

Wonder Woman zigzags in the air, barely escaping Scylla's razor-sharp teeth.

ROAR! The monster's other five heads bellow with anger.

Just then, a scream makes both Scylla and Wonder Woman look up.

Above, a little girl watches them from a small window in the Statue of Liberty's crown. The child looks terrified and can't stop screaming. The girl's mother quickly pulls her away from the window.

Scylla's six heads smile with hungry delight. The creature drags its massive body closer to the statue. It stretches one of its long necks toward the crown. Terrified screams can be heard within as the frightened mother and daughter call out for help.

WHOMP!

Wonder Woman lands with a thud directly in front of Scylla. The Amazon warrior draws her silver sword from the sheath on her back. Her weapon glints in the sunlight.

Turn to page 103.

I need to take the Cyclops to Themyscira before it wakes up, she thinks.

Suddenly, the creature's eye pops wide open. The Cyclops reaches forward and wraps one giant hand around Wonder Woman's waist. The creature lifts the hero off the ground.

The Amazon struggles to free herself as the Cyclops tightens its grip around her. She swings her sword through the air, but the creature is out of reach.

The Cyclops opens its mouth hungrily.

Wonder Woman gasps with pain as the creature tightens its grip. She pushes her sword forward, but the Cyclops is too far away. Her eyes close, and her body goes limp. The sword drops from her hand and falls to the ground.

The Cyclops smiles in triumph. It has defeated the Amazon, and now it will finish her off.

It pulls back its other arm, preparing to deliver a final blow.

Turn to page 98.

Just then, Wonder Woman's eyes pop open.
She reaches for the tiara atop her head and pulls
it from her hair.

The Cyclops blinks its eye in surprise.

WHOOSH! WHOOSH! WHOOSH!

Wonder Woman spins the glittering headpiece
in her hand. The tiara twirls around and around.
It becomes a golden blur.

ZIIIP!

Wonder Woman tosses the tiara, and it goes
flying through the air. The golden tiara smashes
into the Cyclops's head. The creature yells in pain
and falls to the ground. Wonder Woman escapes
from his grasp.

The Amazon lands on the ground next to the
monster. She grabs her sword and then quickly
unfurls her golden lasso. She loops it around
the Cyclops, binding the monster so tightly that
it cannot move. The creature glares at Wonder
Woman as it strains to free itself.

"Struggle all you want, but you're not going anywhere," she says to the monster.

Wonder Woman pauses for a moment and then adds, "Actually, you *are* going someplace. You're going right back behind Doom's Doorway!"

THE END

To follow another path, turn to page 12.

The military planes zoom closer to Ares. The God of War stands on a city street with his arms crossed over his chest.

BLAM! BLAM! BLAM! BLAM!

The military jets fire a dozen missiles. Ares laughs with anticipation.

At the last moment, Wonder Woman swoops her Invisible Jet between Ares and the missiles. The heat-seeking rockets suddenly change course as they lock onto the Amazon's aircraft.

It worked, thinks Wonder Woman. *Now to lead the missiles out of the city.*

The hero pilots her Invisible Jet out over the harbor, performs a loop, and heads straight for the water. Just before she reaches the surface, she pulls up and zooms back into the sky.

SPLOOSH!

The missiles, unable to turn in time, splash down and sink harmlessly into the muddy harbor floor.

Ares roars with rage.

"You are very brave inside your invisible plane," taunts Ares. "But let's see how brave you are without it!"

Ares savagely swings his giant arm where he thinks Wonder Woman's Invisible Jet is flying.

CRUNCH!

The God of War grasps the Amazon's vehicle and crumples it within his fingers.

Wonder Woman ejects from the cockpit and becomes visible once again. She tumbles out of the damaged jet and lands in a crouch at the edge of the harbor. She stares down at the ground, gathering her strength.

With a cruel laugh, Ares steps closer to Wonder Woman.

"The battle is over, Amazon!" he declares.

Ares's eyes begin to glow bright red. The God of War has the power to shoot deadly laser beams from his eyes.

ZAAAAP! Ares blasts Wonder Woman with a molten-hot laser beam!

Turn the page.

Wonder Woman jumps to her feet and crosses her wrists. The lasers bounce off her silver bracelets and blast back toward Ares.

KER-BLAM!

A deafening explosion shakes the ground. A burst of black smoke blinds Wonder Woman for a moment. When the smoke clears, the ground where Ares stood is empty. The God of War has vanished.

Wonder Woman sighs with relief. She then looks behind her. The broken and jagged remains of her Invisible Jet float in the harbor.

"I hope the flight engineers on Themyscira aren't too upset when they see what happened to my jet," she says with a sigh.

THE END

To follow another path, turn to page 12.

"You will go no farther, Scylla!" declares Wonder Woman.

The monster's six squirming heads turn and hiss at the hero.

Suddenly, one of Scylla's heads reaches out and grasps Wonder Woman's sword in its mouth. The Amazon holds onto the sword tightly.

Just then, another of Scylla's heads lunges toward the Amazon. Wonder Woman jumps backward and loses her balance. She falls to the ground. In those few precious seconds, Scylla pulls the sword from Wonder Woman's hand and tosses it into the harbor.

Wonder Woman tries to stand up, but Scylla's angry heads keep darting around the hero. The Amazon rolls from side to side to dodge each angry strike.

The monster inches closer, and its mouths open wide in anticipation. The crowd within the statue screams even louder.

Turn the page.

SPLASH!

Something is happening in the harbor. Scylla and Wonder Woman turn to see what it is.

Aquaman now stands at the edge of Liberty Island. The super hero, who is also the King of the Seven Seas, holds Wonder Woman's sword high above his head.

"Diana, I believe this belongs to you," he says as he tosses the weapon toward Wonder Woman.

The Amazon warrior launches herself into the air and grasps the sword.

Scylla howls in anger.

Wonder Woman soars above Scylla. The hero lifts her sword and swings it through the air as a warning.

"Scylla, the choice is yours," says Wonder Woman. "Travel to Doom's Doorway or face the blade of my Amazonian sword."

Scylla lowers its six heads in defeat. The creature slowly backs away from the Statue of Liberty.

ZIIIP!

Wonder Woman unfurls her golden lasso and quickly loops it around Scylla. The hero uses her superhuman strength to easily lift the massive monster into the air.

As the Amazon warrior carries Scylla over the Statue of Liberty, she notices the famous quote on the statue's plaque. It reads: "Give me your tired, your poor, your huddled masses yearning to breathe free."

Wonder Woman smiles.

"It's a good thing it doesn't say anything about sea monsters!" she says.

THE END

To follow another path, turn to page 12.

AUTHOR

Steve Korté is the author of many books for children and young adults. As a former editor at DC Comics, he worked on hundreds of books featuring Superman, Batman, Wonder Woman, and the other heroes and villains of the DC Universe. He lives in New York City with his husband Bill and his super-cat Duke.

ILLUSTRATOR

Omar Lozano lives in Monterrey, Mexico. He has always been crazy for illustration and is constantly on the lookout for awesome things to draw. In his free time, he watches lots of movies, reads fantasy and sci-fi books, and draws! Omar has worked for Marvel, DC, IDW, Capstone, and several other publishing companies.

GLOSSARY

appetite (AP-uh-tite)—desire for food or drink

bystander (BYE-stan-dur)—someone who is at a place where something happens to someone else

cockpit (KOK-pit)—the area in the front of a plane where the pilot sits

conquer (KAHNG-kuhr)—to defeat and take control of an enemy

fuse (FYOOZ)—to join together

javelin (JAV-uh-luhn)—a light, metal spear that is thrown for distance in a track-and-field event

ricochet (RIK-uh-shay)—to hit a hard surface and go in a different direction

saliva (suh-LYE-vuh)—the clear liquid in the mouth

trident (TRY-dent)—a long spear with three sharp points at its end

typhoon (tie-FOON)—a hurricane that forms in the western Pacific Ocean

unconscious (uhn-KON-shuhss)—not awake; not able to see, feel, or think

waterspout (WAW-tur-spowt)—a mass of spinning cloud-filled wind that stretches from a cloud to a body of water; waterspouts force up a strong spray of water in lakes and oceans

ARES

Real Name:
Ares

Occupation:
God of War

Base:
Mount Olympus

Height:
6 feet 11 inches

Weight:
495 pounds

Eyes:
Blue

Hair:
Blonde

Powers/Abilities:
Immortality, unmatched strength, shape-shifting, teleportation, and indestructible armor. He is also a skilled military leader and strategist.

Although his father is Zeus, the King of the Gods, Ares has never fit in on Mount Olympus. From an early age, he vowed to conquer Earth and overtake the human race. As the God of War, he thrives on conflict and enjoys manipulating humans into fighting with one another. With the powers of teleportation, shape-shifting, and incredible strength, Ares excels at causing chaos and destruction across the globe. Thankfully, Earth has Wonder Woman on its side, born to stop Ares's threats of treachery and death.

- One trait Ares prizes the most is that the larger a conflict grows, the more his powers increase. The villain relishes this trait so much he once had a weapon built for him that could mimic it. The Annihilator was a self-propelled battlesuit that fed on human rage.

- The God of War has several children, each with their own evil powers. Phobos, the God of Fear, can turn any nightmare into a reality. Deimos, the God of Terror, has a beard of snakes with panic-inducing venom. And Eris, the Goddess of Strife, can fill the hearts of her victims with hatred with just a bite of her Golden Apple of Discord.

- Ares might be Zeus's son, but Wonder Woman counters him with powers she received from several goddesses. Demeter granted the Amazon strength and Aphrodite gave her beauty and a loving heart. In addition, Athena allowed her to talk to animals and Hermes granted her speed and flight. With these superpowers, Wonder Woman is Ares's most powerful foe.

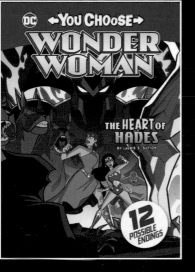

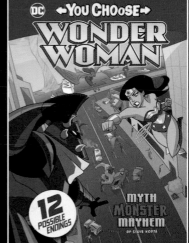

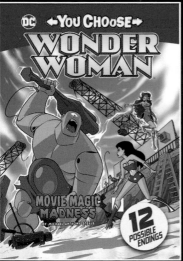

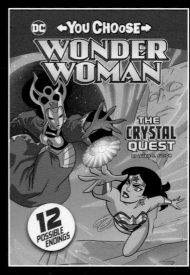